BOOK TWO

A Story About Trusting God

Chattaboonga's Chilling Choice

by SHEILA WALSH

illustrations by DON SULLIVAN

A CHILDREN OF FAITH BOOK *published by* WATERBROOK PRESS

CHATTABOONGA'S CHILLING CHOICE
PUBLISHED BY WATERBROOK PRESS
2375 Telstar Drive, Suite 160
Colorado Springs, Colorado 80920
A division of Random House, Inc.

ISBN 1-57856-334-8

Published in association with the literary agency of Alive Communications, Inc.,
7680 Goddard Street, Suite 200, Colorado Springs, CO 80920.

The executive producer of Gnoo Zoo is Stephen Arterburn, M.Ed.

Printed in the United States of America
2001—First Edition

10 9 8 7 6 5 4 3 2 1

"You will find the True Gnoo Key when you continue your journey—if you choose to go. Then you can return and help those left behind on the carousel.

"I must warn you, little ones: The journey from here will be more difficult than ever. But I will always be with you. So tell me: Who will go?"

—*In Search of the Great White Tiger*

Chattaboonga and her four friends were on a mission for the Great White Tiger.

"Come on, everybody!" she cried as they swung across a canyon. "Keep up! What an adventure!"

"Wait for us!" Big Billy shouted.

"How do I look with the wind in my feathers?" Miss Marbles asked.

"Like a f...mm, a f...mm...a flying mattress," Einstein said, his mouth full of his favorite chocolate bar.

"Aahhrrghh!" Miss Marbles shrieked. "Heeeelp!"

Chattaboonga swung back to free her frazzled feathered friend, whose purse was tangled in a vine.

"We can't lose this," she said, pulling the Great White Tiger's instructions from Miss Marbles's purse.

> *On the next part of your journey,*
> *stay together, come what may.*
> *I will keep you safe from danger.*
> *Let my pawprints lead the way.*

"What kind of danger?" asked Chattaboonga.

Suddenly something grabbed her tail! Frightened, she quickly wriggled free and hurried to her friends.

"I...I think Reptillion is following us!" Chattaboonga told Big Billy. Her excitement for adventure had vanished.

"The Great White Tiger told us to look out for him," Big Billy reminded her. "That's why we must stick together."

"Well, he didn't stop Reptillion from snatching Boongachatta!" she said, looking over at her twin sister.

"But he kept her safe," Big Billy said.

"So what's...the...plan?" a breathless Einstein asked as the group pulled themselves up a steep, rocky hillside, leaving the canyon behind.

"We must find the key and return to the Gnoo Zoo," said Big Billy.

"Not me!" said Chattaboonga. "Let the other animals free themselves. We did!"

"They need our help," Big Billy reminded her. "We had help too, remember?"

"It's not safe!" Chattaboonga said. "I'm not going to risk my life looking for a dumb key. I'm going to hide!"

"Chattaboonga, the only safe way is his way," Billy said.

"Over here!" Miss Marbles interrupted them. "Our instructions said, 'Let my pawprints lead the way.' Well, look!" Jumping with excitement, her pearls bouncing, she pointed to large, deep pawprints that led into a mysterious forest.

"I'm not going into that dark place!" Chattaboonga cried. She pointed to a lovely field in the opposite direction of the forest. "Boongachatta! Look at the monkeys playing over there—let's go!"

"No!" said Big Billy. "We must stay together."

"If you stay with us, I'll...I'll...I'll share some of my chocolate with you," Einstein offered.

Chattaboonga did not want chocolate. She wanted to protect herself from Reptillion.

Big Billy began to follow the pawprints, leading the group toward the dark forest. Chattaboonga would not go.

"Listen! Listen!" she screeched, jumping up and down. "I think I can hear Reptillion in there!"

She turned on her tail and ran away as fast as she could.

"Chattaboonga!" her sister cried.

But it was too late. Chattaboonga had run off to the field of flowers.

Faster and faster, Chattaboonga ran toward the dancing monkeys.

"Hi!" she said happily. "Mind if I crash your party?"

But her happiness turned to terror when she saw that the monkeys weren't monkeys at all!

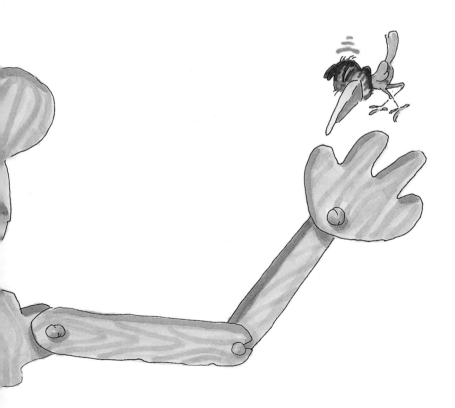

"There's always room for *food!*" Reptillion screamed, snatching Chattaboonga by the tail. "There's no escape for you! No one to hear your sniveling little cries!"

"Help! Help me, Great White Tiger!" Chattaboonga cried, tears streaming down her face.

"I say, old girl—up here!"

Chattaboonga looked up and saw her old friend Toodaloo flying above her head.

"Toodaloo, help me!" she sobbed.

"Righty-o! Emergency procedures!"

He flew down and took Chattaboonga's hand, dodging Reptillion's attempts to knock him out of the sky. "Now roar! As loudly as you can!" he told her. "Roar in the name of the Great White Tiger!"

The small monkey and the small mouse lifted their voices, but what came out was...

...the roar of the Great White Tiger himself!

"Aahhrrghh!" Reptillion screamed and dropped Chattaboonga. "Stop that noise!"

"Come now, Chattaboonga," Toodaloo said. "They will only be deaf for moments. Have you ever flown before, old girl?"

"Not really," Chattaboonga replied.

"Well, get ready for your first real flight!"

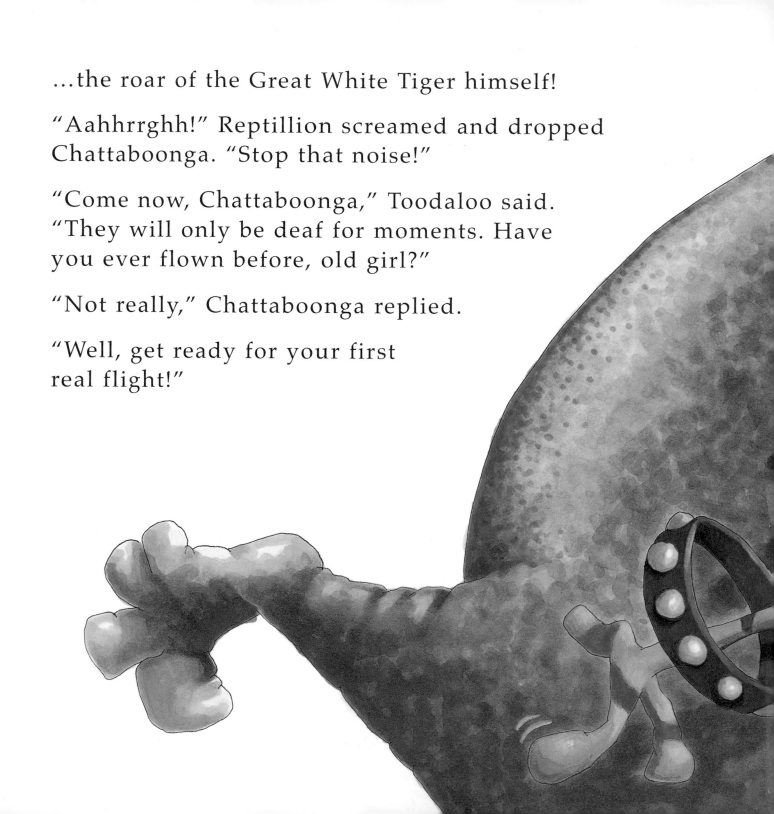

Chattaboonga held on to Toodaloo's tail, and soon they were soaring high over the field.

"Yahoo! I'm flying!" Chattaboonga called. She was much less afraid of flying than she was of Reptillion. "Hey, look at Reptillion! He looks so small from up here!"

"Righty-o," said Toodaloo. "That's how the Great White Tiger sees him too."

"I have something to show you, Chattaboonga," Toodaloo said.

They flew and flew until they were high over the Gnoo Zoo. Chattaboonga could see the gloomy faces of the animals who were stuck to their carousel poles.

"They look so unhappy," Chattaboonga said with sadness in her voice.

"Every time someone leaves the Gnoo Zoo, Reptillion makes life even more miserable for those left behind," Toodaloo told her. "Now you know why you must find the key and go back. The key will unlock the carousel forever, and all the animals will finally be free."

Chattaboonga was thoughtful as they flew away in the light of the golden Gnoo moon.

Soon Chattaboonga could see her friends.

"Look, Toodaloo. There they are!"

Big Billy and the others were near the dark forest. Toodaloo set her down gently.

"You're back!" Boongachatta cried. "We were so worried. What happened?"

"Oh, it's too much to tell now. We have to find the key and go back," Chattaboonga replied.

"I think we should have found the key by now," Einstein said.

"You will only find it together," Toodaloo said.

He gave a small red box to Chattaboonga. "Take this," he said. "Now I must be off. Toodle pip!" Then he was gone.

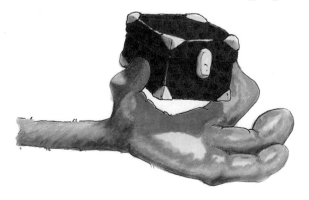

"I'm sorry I didn't stay with you," Chattaboonga said. "Now I know that even when scary things happen the Great White Tiger is with us. Those woods can't scare me now!"

"What's in the box?" Einstein asked. "Chocolate?"

Chattaboonga opened it carefully. Nestled inside the box were four candy hammers.

"How can they fit into such a tiny box?" Miss Marbles said. Chattaboonga wondered the same thing.

"The Great White Tiger is full of surprises," Big Billy said. "No doubt we'll need those hammers on the next part of our journey! But now there's no time to lose. Are we set?"

"To find the key!" Chattaboonga cried.

"To find the key!" her friends echoed.

And the happy little band marched into the dark woods.

Learn how Chattaboonga and her friends began their journey and met the Great White Tiger in Book One of the Gnoo Zoo series, *In Search of the Great White Tiger.*

Where will their adventures take them next? Keep an eye open in 2002 for Book Three, *Einstein's Enormous Error,* in which the travelers learn an important lesson about extending forgiveness to one another.

In Gnoo Zoo Book Four, *Miss Marbles's Marvelous Makeover,* pride gets in the way of her wisdom and almost costs the vain ostrich her life. But the ever-gracious mercy of the Great White Tiger restores her to the group as they continue their important mission.

More Gnoo Zoo and Children of Faith products are coming soon!